# HANSEL
## AND
# GRETEL

Pictures by T. IZAWA and S. HIJIKATA

GROSSET & DUNLAP • Publishers • NEW YORK

A NATIONAL GENERAL COMPANY

In a humble cottage in a forest there lived a poor woodchopper with his wife and two children, Hansel and Gretel. There wasn't much to eat, even in good times, but at last the day came when there was no food at all.

That night, after the children had gone to bed, the woodchopper said, "What will become of us? How can we live without food?"

ISBN: 0-448-04239-8
Illustrations Copyright © 1967, 1971 by Tadasu Izawa and Shigemi Hijikata
through management of Dairisha, Inc. Printed and bound in Japan
by Zokeisha Publications, Ltd., Roppongi, Minato-ku, Tokyo.

His wife, who had an unkind heart, replied, "Tomorrow we'll take the children into the deepest woods, and leave them. Then we will have only two mouths to feed."

Now, the children, who had been too hungry to sleep, heard this, and Gretel began to cry. "Dear Hansel," she moaned, "what shall we do?"

Hansel tried to comfort his sister. "Don't be afraid," he said.
"I have a plan that will help us to find our way back home."

Early the next morning the children were awakened. "Come,"
said the mother, "we must all go into the woods to find food."
Hansel brought along a crust of stale bread that he had found and

dropped tiny crumbs along the path so that they could find their way home again.

When they reached the deepest part of the forest, the mother told the children to lie down to rest. While Hansel and Gretel dozed in the warm sunlight, she and her husband slipped back through the forest to the cottage.

The tired, hungry children were soon fast asleep. When night came, their guardian angels hovered over them to keep them from harm.

In the morning, when they awoke, Hansel went to look for the trail of bread crumbs. Alas! the forest birds had eaten every one. So Hansel and Gretel wandered this way and that through the woods, looking for berries to eat.

Suddenly, ahead of them in a clearing, they saw a house made of gingerbread and cakes and candies! Joyfully they rushed up to the house and began to eat whatever they could break off.

At that moment an old woman appeared. She smiled sweetly and invited Hansel and Gretel into her house for a proper meal. What delicious food they had to eat! The children ate until they could hold no more. Then the woman tucked them tenderly into bed for the night.

Now, it so happened that this old woman was a crafty old witch, and she planned to fatten Hansel and Gretel in order to eat them. The next morning she awakened the children with a rough shake, and dragged Hansel off to a cage and locked him up. She made Gretel do all the housework and cooking.

Poor Gretel cried and cried, but it was no use. Each day the best food she cooked was served to Hansel, because the old witch wanted him nice and plump before she ate him.

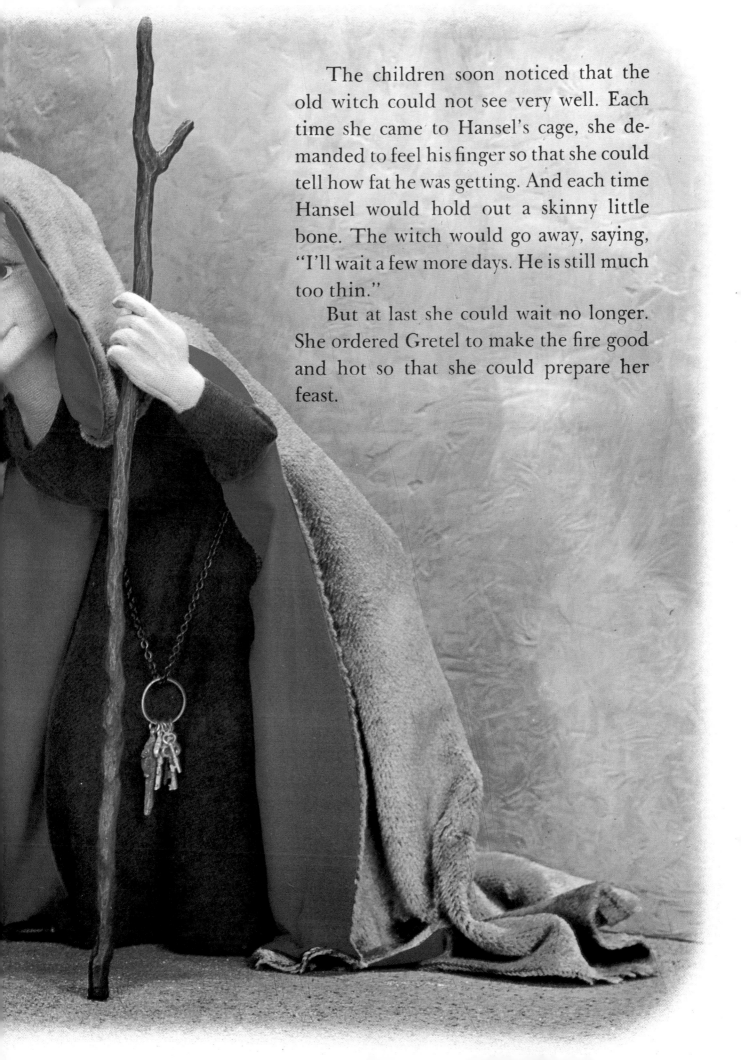

The children soon noticed that the old witch could not see very well. Each time she came to Hansel's cage, she demanded to feel his finger so that she could tell how fat he was getting. And each time Hansel would hold out a skinny little bone. The witch would go away, saying, "I'll wait a few more days. He is still much too thin."

But at last she could wait no longer. She ordered Gretel to make the fire good and hot so that she could prepare her feast.

With a sad heart the little girl started a hot fire in the oven. Soon the witch bustled into the kitchen, asking how the fire was coming along.

"I cannot tell," answered Gretel. "I have never made such a large fire before."

"Out of my way, foolish girl!" said the impatient witch. "I will see for myself."

As she opened the door and leaned forward to look, Gretel gave the wicked witch a tremendous push. Into the fire she tumbled! Gretel quickly shut the heavy door and ran to free her brother.

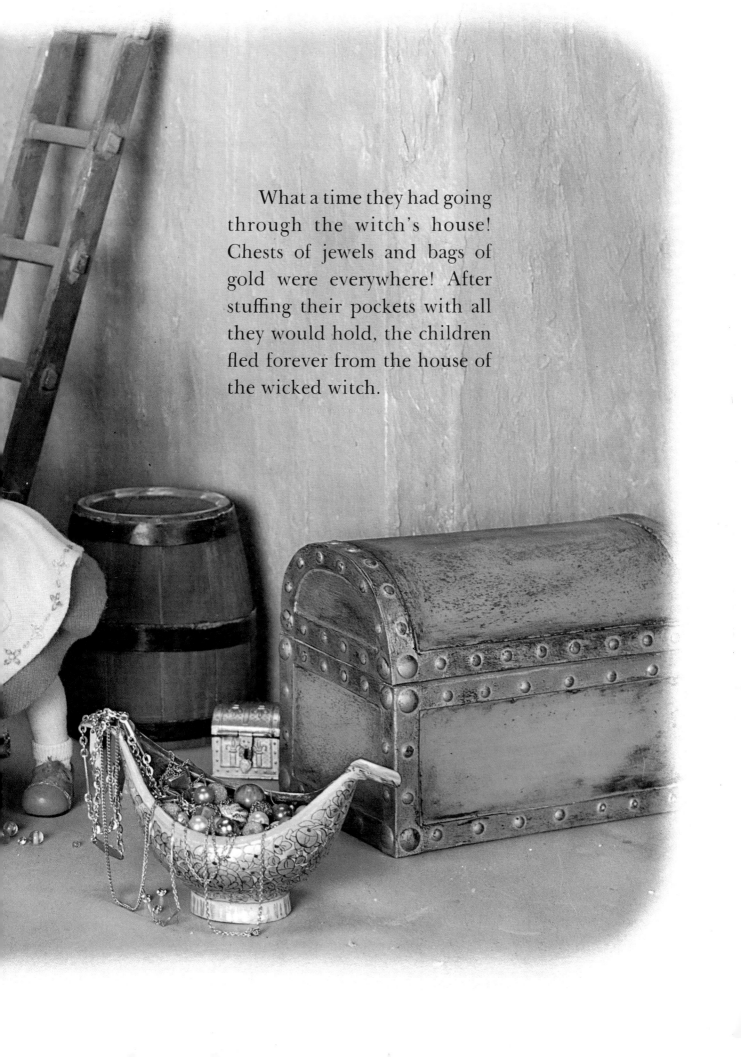

What a time they had going through the witch's house! Chests of jewels and bags of gold were everywhere! After stuffing their pockets with all they would hold, the children fled forever from the house of the wicked witch.

They presently came to a lake, and seeing no way to cross, the children gave up hope of ever getting home. But soon a white swan appeared, and offered to carry them across the lake on his back. When they arrived on the other shore, who should be there cutting wood but their father! He was overjoyed to see his beloved children again, and the children lost no time in showing him their treasures.

After thanking the swan for his help, Hansel and Gretel and the woodchopper returned to live happily once more in their cottage in the woods.